# DAVID A. ADLER

*Pictures by Lloyd Bloom*

VOYAGER BOOKS
HARCOURT BRACE & COMPANY

*San Diego    New York    London*

*For Al Lipson and the scores*
*of other survivors who have shared their*
*memories with me*
—D. A. A.


*To my wife, Shulamit*
—L. B.

Text copyright © 1995 by David A. Adler
Illustrations copyright © 1995 by Lloyd Bloom

Requests for permission to make copies of any part of the work should
be mailed to: Permissions Department, Harcourt Brace & Company,
6277 Sea Harbor Drive, Orlando, Florida 32887-6777.

First Voyager Books edition 1999
*Voyager Books* is a registered trademark of Harcourt Brace & Company.

The Library of Congress has cataloged the hardcover edition as follows:
Adler, David A.
One yellow daffodil: a Hanukkah story/David A. Adler; illustrated
by Lloyd Bloom.—1st ed.
p. cm.
Summary: During Hanukkah two children help a Holocaust survivor to
once again embrace his religious traditions.
ISBN 0-15-200537-4
ISBN 0-15-202094-2 pb
[1. Hanukkah—Fiction.  2. Holocaust survivors—Fiction.
3. Florists—Fiction.  4. Jews—United States—Fiction.]
I. Bloom, Lloyd, ill.  II. Title.
PZ7.A2615On  1995
[Fic]—dc20    94-31374

C E F D

Printed in Singapore

The illustrations in this book were done in liquitex acrylic on
Saunders Waterford watercolor paper.
The display type was set in Nicolas Cochin Italic.
The text type was set in Columbus by Thompson Type, San Diego, California.
Color separations by Bright Arts, Ltd., Singapore
Printed and bound by Tien Wah Press, Singapore
This book was printed on Arctic matte paper.
Production supervision by Stanley Redfern and Jane Van Gelder
Designed by Lisa Peters

MORRIS KAPLAN IS a fictional character
inspired by many of the Holocaust survivors
I interviewed while researching previous
books. Many survivors told me that after the
war they returned to their villages, as Morris
did, hoping to find a relative or friend who
had survived. Many told me, too, that after
the war they felt an emptiness that would
not go away. —D. A. A.

Morris Kaplan lives in a small apartment above a busy restaurant. Every evening the muffled sounds of tables being set, music, people talking and laughing keep Morris company while he prepares and eats his dinner, and as he reads the evening newspaper. Morris often falls asleep in his chair by the window, with the open newspaper spread across his legs like a blanket. He sleeps there through the night, still dressed in his robe and slippers.

Morris wakes early each morning, even before milk and vegetables are delivered to the restaurant. He dresses carefully and has his breakfast of toast, jelly, and tea in a glass. Then Morris goes outside, starts his small pickup truck, and begins the long drive to the flower market.

This morning at the market Morris walks slowly among the large buckets filled with irises, daisies, carnations, roses, and lilies. He takes deep breaths of the fragrant air. At one stand Morris picks up a red carnation. He brushes his hand softly over its petals, examines its stem and leaves. He will select only the freshest and prettiest flowers for his shop.

Morris looks around. The buckets, stands, and walls are dull and gray. Most of the people are wearing dark suits or aprons. Only the flowers add color to the market. As he stands there, Morris remembers a time, long ago, when everything around him was dark and sad. One spring morning he saw a bright yellow flower growing in a most unlikely place. That flower gave him hope and courage. Morris believes that flower saved his life.

Morris wipes away a tear and walks to another stand. This one has buckets of roses. Morris picks up a red rose, smells it. Then he shakes it gently.

An hour later the back of Morris's truck is filled with flowers. He drives to his shop and carries them in.

It's still very early. Only a few people walk past the shop. Morris tears a sheet of wrapping paper from a thick roll and lays it on his desk. He places a few sprigs of baby's breath on the paper, then some pink and red carnations. He wraps the flowers and puts the arrangement into a bucket. Then he tears off a new sheet of wrapping paper.

When the bucket is full, Morris puts today's arrangements and the rest of the flowers he bought at the market in the glass-doored refrigerator.

Outside, more people walk past his shop. Children pass by on their way to school. Morris stands by the door of his shop to watch them.

"Oh, Mr. Kaplan," a boy and girl call to him. "Good morning. Good morning, Mr. Kaplan."

Morris waves to the children. The girl runs to him. "We're late today. We can't stop and talk, but we'll be back later, on our way home."

Morris smiles. "I know," he says. "Today is Friday. I'll see you this afternoon."

Morris watches them hurry off. He waits outside until he can no longer see them. Then he goes back into the shop.

Soon a woman walks in. "I want something pretty," she says, "for my husband. It's his birthday today."

Morris opens the refrigerator door. He shows her the arrangements, the buckets of roses, carnations, and chrysanthemums.

"I'll take one dozen carnations," she says. "Can you mix reds and whites?"

The woman looks at the many vases and plants in the shop while Morris arranges the flowers. He takes out six red, six white, and six pink carnations. He tears off a sheet of wrapping paper and adds some baby's breath.

"Oh my," the woman says. "I only wanted a dozen flowers."

Morris smiles. "The red and white flowers are a birthday gift from you. The pink ones are from me."

In the early afternoon, children begin to return from school. The girl and boy Morris had spoken to earlier walk in.

"Hi, Mr. Kaplan," the girl says.

"Hello, Ilana. Hello, Jonathan."

"My class had a test today in math," Ilana says, "on fractions. It was hard. And we had a spelling test. That was easy."

Ilana takes a small purse from her knapsack. "We need some flowers," she says. "We only have two dollars left from our allowances, so could we have some of your old flowers? They're just for tonight and tomorrow."

"I know," Morris says, and smiles. "They have to look nice for the Sabbath."

*"Shabbat,"* Ilana says.

"Yes, *Shabbat."*

Morris opens the refrigerator and takes out one of the arrangements he made this morning. He puts it on his desk and tears open the wrapping paper. He goes back to the refrigerator and takes out some red, pink, and white carnations and some chrysanthemums and adds them to the arrangement. He wraps them all in fresh paper and gives the flowers to Ilana.

"These are a lot of flowers for two dollars," she says as she gives Morris the money.

Morris smiles. "When you buy old flowers, you get more."

It's December and darkness comes early. Morris stays in his shop until long after nightfall. Before he leaves he checks the flowers that remain. There are plenty for tomorrow. *That's good. Saturday is always a busy day.*

Morris drives his truck home. He lives close enough to the shop to walk, but he likes to have the truck with him, just in case. In the almost forty years that Morris has lived in his apartment and worked in his flower shop, he has never had to rush off somewhere. Still, he likes to have the truck nearby.

Snow falls through Sunday night. Monday morning, on his way to the flower shop, Morris listens to radio reports about the weather, the condition of the roads, and school closings. Ilana and Jonathan's school is open. Morris is glad. He looks forward to seeing them.

Morris makes the flower arrangements and then goes outside in time to see the children on their way to school.

The next day, in the afternoon, Jonathan and Ilana come into Morris's shop. "We'd like to buy some flowers," Ilana says.

"Isn't today Tuesday?" Morris asks.

"Yes."

"But you always buy flowers for the Sabbath. The Sabbath doesn't begin until Friday night."

Ilana smiles. "I know, but tonight is the first night of Hanukkah."

Morris opens the glass refrigerator door. "Look here. See what you like."

"We only have five dollars," Ilana says.

"You just pick the flowers you want. When you have picked five dollars' worth, I'll say 'Stop.'"

Ilana and Jonathan pick flowers for a large bouquet. Morris wraps it and gives the flowers to Ilana.

"Don't you celebrate Hanukkah?" Jonathan asks.

"No."

"Do you celebrate Christmas?"

"No," Morris says softly. "I don't celebrate either holiday. When I was a small boy in Poland, I celebrated Hanukkah, but that was many years ago."

After the children leave the shop, Morris sits by his desk and thinks of his Hanukkahs in Poland. It was long ago that he was in school, that he studied the Talmud and other holy books. He remembers helping his father in his tailor shop, lighting candles on Hanukkah, and getting a few coins, Hanukkah *gelt,* as a gift. Morris thinks of his parents, his brother, and two sisters—and of what happened to them.

The next afternoon Ilana and Jonathan come into his shop again.

"Oh my," Morris says when the children walk in. "You bought so many flowers yesterday. You can't want more already. They didn't wilt, did they?"

"Oh no," Ilana says. "The flowers are fine. They're beautiful. But Mamma said we should invite you to come to our apartment tonight to eat dinner and to light Hanukkah candles with us."

"I can't. I have to stay here in the shop."

"Mamma says you can come after you close the shop."

Morris shakes his head. "No, that would be too late. I close the shop at eight."

"That's fine. We wait for Pappa to come home from work, and that's after eight."

Before Morris can object again, Ilana writes her address and apartment number on a slip of paper and says to Morris, "We'll wait for you, too."

After the children leave, Morris looks around the shop. He wants to bring a gift, but the family already has flowers. Morris takes a ceramic bowl off the shelf and puts it on his desk. It's a beautiful bowl. He looks at the bowl a long time. Then he shakes his head. "We are both the same," he says. *"Empty.* I must find a nice plant for you."

Morris puts a pot of ivy into the bowl. He ties a blue bow to the plant. He begins to write a card, "Dear Mr. and Mrs. . . ." But he doesn't know the children's family name. He takes another card and writes: "Thank you for inviting me to dinner. Morris Kaplan."

That evening Morris closes his shop a little early. He goes home, shaves, and changes his shirt. He takes the ivy in the ceramic bowl and drives to the address on the slip of paper. Ilana and Jonathan live in apartment 2C. The name on the door is Becker. Morris knocks.

"Come in, come in," Mrs. Becker says as she opens the door. "You must be Mr. Kaplan."

Morris gives her the ivy. He looks around the apartment. There are flowers everywhere.

"You gave the children so many," Mrs. Becker says. "We couldn't possibly fit them all in one vase."

Ilana and Jonathan are by the window. Jonathan holds a box of multicolored candles and is giving them, one by one, to Ilana.

"I want mine to be blue tonight," he tells Ilana, and hands her three blue candles. She sets them in Jonathan's menorah, one in each of the first two holders at the right, and one in the raised holder in the center.

"What color do you want?" Jonathan asks Morris.

"I'll just watch."

"We put this menorah out for you. It's extra," Jonathan says.

"No. I'll just watch."

Just as Ilana and Jonathan finish preparing the menorahs, their father arrives. He introduces himself to Morris. Then everyone gathers near the window. First Mr. Becker says the blessings and lights his candles, then Mrs. Becker, then Ilana, and then Jonathan. Together they sing "Ha-Nerut Hallalu" (These Candles) and "Ma'oz Zur" (Rock of Ages).

While the candles burn, they all play a game of dreidel. They each put a chocolate-covered raisin in the middle of the table and then take turns spinning the dreidel to see who wins the candy. When Jonathan isn't spinning, he's eating.

"Let's have dinner now," Mrs. Becker says, "before Jonathan eats every raisin in the game."

At dinner Morris talks on and on about flowers. His favorite is the hyacinth. "I fill a glass bowl with pebbles and set a hyacinth bulb on top. I keep the pebbles wet. When the bulb blooms, I just enjoy its color, beauty, and fragrance."

"Were you always interested in flowers?" Mrs. Becker asks.

Morris looks down at his plate and says, "No. When I was young, we didn't have flowers at our table. My parents were too busy to think about such things, and we were too poor."

Morris looks up. "I wanted to be a tailor, like my father. He had magic hands. They could take a drab piece of flat cloth and make from it a wedding suit. But war came, and I no longer thought of cloth and suits."

"Were you in the army?" Jonathan asks.

"No."

"Did you see soldiers fighting?"

"No."

"Jonathan, don't ask so many questions," Mrs. Becker says.

While the children talk about school, Morris thinks about the Hanukkahs he celebrated many years ago.

After dessert Morris thanks the Beckers and leaves. At home he searches in his closet. He brings out an old box. Inside are a metal cup, a torn shirt, a child's hat, and an old menorah. Morris holds the menorah in both hands and cries.

The next morning Morris takes the menorah with him to the flower shop. He cleans it and puts it in the window. He looks at it often during the day.

That night, after Morris closes the shop, he puts the menorah on the front seat of his truck. As he drives, he remembers the last time he used the menorah. His sister had helped him. It was just before the Nazis came to his village and took him and his family away to a ghetto. Later they were taken by train to Auschwitz.

Morris remembers the horrors of that place. He remembers when he was separated from his family.

One morning, after he had lost all hope of survival, Morris saw a small yellow flower, a daffodil, blooming just outside his barracks. The rain he had cursed because of the mud it made had nurtured the flower. Now it was reaching out for the sun. *If the daffodil can survive here*, Morris thought, *maybe I can, too.* Morris knows that luck, more than anything, saved him. But he feels the flower saved him, too.

Morris stops for a red light and realizes that he isn't driving home. He is at the Beckers' building. He parks the truck, takes his menorah, and goes in. He stands quietly outside apartment 2C for a while. He looks at the menorah and then knocks on the door.

"Mr. Kaplan! Come in." Mrs. Becker greets him.

"This is the menorah I used when I was young," Morris tells her.

Morris sits at the table and tells the Beckers about the family he lost and about the yellow daffodil.

"After the war I didn't know where to go, so I went home," he says. "Another family was living in our house. They were using our furniture, our pots and dishes, and wearing our clothing. They were not happy to see me, but they did give me a small box of things that they didn't want. Our menorah was in that box."

There are tears in Morris's eyes. "I thought maybe I would find some of my old friends in the village, but I didn't. I had no one."

Mrs. Becker holds Morris's hand in hers and says, "Now you have us."

Morris puts his menorah by the window. Jonathan gives Ilana four candles. She sets them in the menorah. The Beckers listen as Morris says the blessings and watch as he lights the Hanukkah candles.

נֵר ה׳ נִשְׁמַת אָדָם
מִשְׁלֵי כ כז

The soul of man is a candle of God . . .
—Proverbs 20.27